Livelytime
PLAYSONGS

Baby's active day in
songs and pictures

Compiled by **Sheena Roberts**

Illustrated by **Rachel Fuller**

Performed by **Sandra Kerr**, **Leon Rosselson** and **Janet Russell**

A & C BLACK · LONDON · ... SONGS PUBLICATIONS LTD

Moon to bed and sun to skies

upsy daisy, time to rise!

Sally go round the sun

Sally go round the sun,
Sally go round the moon,
Sally go round the chimney pots,
On a Saturday afternoon ~ HEY!

Ring a ring a roses

Ring a ring a roses,
A pocketful of posies,
Atishoo, atishoo,
We all fall down.

Picking up the daisies,
Picking up the daisies,
Atishoo, atishoo,
We all jump up.

Sally go round the sun

Little babies+
● Pat her back in time to the music as you hold her on your shoulder and walk or rock.

Bigger babies+
● Hold her under the arms and 'skip' her round in a circle. On 'HEY', swing her up in the air, turn and go back the other way.

Ring a ring a roses

Little babies+
● Pat her back as you move in time to the music.

Bigger babies+
● Jog round with her in your arms, or hold baby's hands if she is starting to walk.
■ Drop together to the floor.
▲ Pick up 'daisies' then jump back up again.

Toddlers+
Both these songs are simple, first circle games to play with her friends or bigger sisters and brothers.

Baby is referred to as 'she' throughout these instructions, and as 'he' throughout the instructions in the companion title, Sleepytime Playsongs.

Catch him crow

● Catch him crow,
Carry him kite,

■ Take him away
Till the apples are ripe.

And when they're ripe
And ready to fall,

▲ Down comes baby,
Apples and all.

Looby loo

● Here we go looby loo
Here we go looby light,
Here we go looby loo
All on a Saturday night.

■ We jump the baby in
And jump the baby out,
We jingle her here
    and jingle her there,
And bounce her all about.

Here we go looby loo...

■ We tap her ankles in
And tap her ankles out,
We shake them left
    and shake them right,
And bounce her all about.

Here we go looby loo...

▲ We swing the baby in
And swing the baby out,
We swing her up
    and swing her down,
And bounce her all about.

Here we go looby loo...

Catch him crow

Little babies+
● Pat her tummy in time to the rhyme.

Bigger babies+
● Swoop her up from your knee or from the floor.

■ 'Fly' her above your head, bobbing her in time to the rhyme.

▲ Swoop her down again and pat her knees or the floor with pretend apples.

Looby loo

Little babies+
● Pat her back as you move with her in your arms to the bouncy rhythm.

Bigger babies+
Cradle her between your arms, facing outward, and with a leg in each of your hands, then:

● dance to the rhythm of the song;

■ do as the words suggest: shake her legs; tap her ankles to one side then to the other.

▲ Hold her under the arms and swing her in, out and all about.

Peekaboo! I can see you!

Peekaboo

Peekaboo

Little babies+

- When she starts to enjoy peekaboo games, use your hands, a scarf or a piece of her clothing to hide her face while you sing. Uncover her frequently ~ peekaboo games are all about reassurance ~ things and people disappear, but not for long.

  Change 'cradle' to suit your setting.

- Where do you think our baby's hiding,
  Where do you think our baby's hiding,
  Where do you think our baby's hiding,
  Where can the baby be?

  Peekaboo, I can see you,
  Peekaboo, I can see you,
  Peekaboo, I can see you,
  Hiding in your cradle.

  ...Hiding in your push chair.

  ...Hiding in your bath towel.

Peeketty peeketty

Little babies+

- Use your own or baby's hands to make the peekaboo 'door'.

  Alternatively, drift a very light silk or chiffon scarf over her as she lies on her back. Pull it away on 'boo'.

  As her confidence grows, she will like pulling the scarf away herself.

Peeketty peeketty

- Peeketty, peeketty, peeketty boo!
  You can't see me, I can't see you.
  Open the door and let me through,
  Peeketty, peeketty, peeketty ~ BOO!

Here sits a teddy

● Here sits a teddy on your knee, knee, knee,
Hide away, teddy. Where can he be?

Where is he? Where can he be?

■ Boo! There's the teddy, can you see?
Now he wants to clap for the baby!

...Now he wants to dance for the baby!

...Now he wants a kiss from the baby!

Bananas in pyjamas

● Bananas
In pyjamas
Are coming down the stairs,
Bananas
In pyjamas
Are coming down in pairs,
Bananas
In pyjamas
Are chasing teddy bears ~
'Cos on Tuesdays
They all try to
■ Catch them unawares.

Here sits a teddy

Little babies+
As soon as she is focusing on objects, play this little game to capture her attention and curiosity.

● Bounce a teddy on her knee then hide it behind your back.

■ On 'boo', jump teddy back into view to 'clap', 'dance' or 'kiss' baby.

Toddlers+
She'll delight in hiding teddy from you then making him perform the actions.

Bananas in pyjamas

Little babies+
● March your fingers down from head to toes.

■ Catch her up in a hug. When she's bigger, swing her right up in the air.

Spy with your eye ~ and hear with your ear!

I spy with my little eye

I spy with my little eye

I spy with my little eye,
You can hear with your little ear ~
A big yellow bus go beep beep beep,
And we'll all go travelling by,
  bye bye,
And we'll all go travelling by.

I spy with my little eye,
You can hear with your little ear ~
A little blue car go vroom vroom vroom,
A big yellow bus go beep beep beep,
And we'll all go travelling by,
  bye bye,
And we'll all go travelling by.

I spy with my little eye,
You can hear with your little ear ~
An ice cream van go dingalingaling,
A little blue car go vroom vroom vroom,
A big yellow bus go beep beep beep,
And we'll all go travelling by,
  bye bye,
And we'll all go travelling by.

I spy with my little eye

Little babies:
- Rock her on your shoulder or in your arms as you move to the rhythm.

Press her nose every time the bus goes 'beep'. Wave on 'bye bye'.

Toddlers:
- Make circles with index fingers and thumbs to spy through, and cup hands behind ears as you listen. Wave on 'bye bye'.

Sing the colours of other things and make their sounds as you see and hear them while travelling by together.

How many vehicles can you add without forgetting the order?

Here comes the train

Here comes the train ~ whooo whooo,
Very far away ~ whooo whooo,
Huff huff, chink chink, puff puff, rattle rattle,
Huff huff, chink chink, puff puff, rattle rattle.

Here comes the train... will it stop and play?...

Here is the train... going very fast...

There goes the train... rushing straight past...

The wheels on the bus

The wheels on the bus go round and round,
Round and round, round and round,
The wheels on the bus go round and round,
All day long.

The bell on the bus goes ting ting ting,
Ting ting ting, ting ting ting,
The bell on the bus goes ting ting ting,
All day long.

The babies on the bus all clap their hands,
Clap their hands, clap their hands,
The babies on the bus all clap their hands,
All day long.

Here comes the train

Little babies+
- Sit baby on your knee and take her hands in yours to use as pistons. Start quietly and slowly, get faster and louder, then very, very quiet again.

The wheels on the bus

Little babies+
- Rest baby back against your raised knees and do the actions for her ~ make circles with your hands for the wheels going round; 'ring' the bell; clap hands.

  Make up your own verses and actions.
- In her own time, she will start to copy the actions.

Toddlers+
- This is a great first action song for your toddler to play independently, as each verse has only one, simple action.

Find a friend ~

play let's pretend

PLAYGROUP friendly toys

Look who comes here

12

- Look who comes here,
It's a friendly little dolly,
Look who comes here,
It's a friendly little doll.
What can you do for us,
Friendly little dolly?
What can you do for us,
Friendly little doll?
  > Oh, I can tap on your high chair,
  > tap tap tap, tap tap tap,
  > I can tap on your high chair,
  > tap tap tap tap tap.

Look who comes here,
It's a friendly little kitten,
Look who comes here,
It's a friendly little cat...
  > Oh, I can sing a song for you,
  > meow...

Look who comes here,
It's a friendly little froggy,
Look who comes here,
It's a friendly little frog...
  > Oh, I can play my kazoo for you,
  > doo doo doo...

Naughty little monkey

13

- Naughty little monkey,
Hiding up a tree,

Throwing down the coconuts,
■ One two three!

▲ Along came an elephant,
They squashed him flat!

- Naughty little monkey,
Don't do that!

Look who comes here
Little babies+
- Use her favourite toys as puppets to act out the song.

The words are easily changed to suit different toys.

Naughty little monkey
Little babies+
- Jog her in your arms or lightly tap her palms to the beat of the rhyme as she rests against your raised knees.

Bigger babies+
- Bounce her on your knee, facing outward.

■ Clap your hands together on 'one two three' ~ she will copy when ready.

▲ Hold her hands and raise and lower your knees alternately so she sways broadly from side to side as if riding an elephant. Lower both knees suddenly on 'flat'.

Little farmyard

I've got a little farmyard
By a running stream,
I've got a little barnyard
Where the grass is green,
There the hens
All peck like this ~
    peck peck.
There the hens
All peck like this ~
    peck peck.
Peck peck, peck peck,
When I call them to
    come home,
Peck peck, peck peck,
When I call them to
    come home.

I've got a little farmyard...
There the cuckoos
Go like this ~
    cuckoo...

I've got a little farmyard...
There the geese
All hiss like this ~
    hiss hiss...

I've got a little farmyard...
There the ducks
All quack like this ~
    quack quack...

Three little monkeys

● Three little monkeys
  Bouncing on the bed,
■ One fell off
  And bumped his head.
▲ Mummy called the doctor
  And the doctor said,
  No more monkey business,
  Bouncing on the bed!

Two little monkeys
Bouncing on the bed...

One little monkey
Bouncing on the bed...

Little farmyard

Little babies+
● The animal sounds
  will intrigue her.
  Add your own verses
  and sounds.

Bigger babies+
● This is a great knee
  bouncer ~ the pace is
  perfect, and she'll
  soon be joining in
  with the animal
  sounds.

Three little monkeys

Little babies+
● Perform the actions
  for her with a toy
  monkey.

Bigger babies+
● Cover your knees with
  a small blanket and
  bounce her.
■ Part your knees so she
  slips down between
  them supported by
  the blanket.
▲ Pretend to phone,
  then wag a finger at
  her in mock severity.

Jiggety jig
to buy a pink pig

5 ~ 4 ~ 3 2 1

● 5 ~ 4 ~ 3 2 1
This little pony has lots of fun,

■ First jumps up, and then jumps down,
And then goes clip clop off to town.

▲ Clip clop, clip clop, clip clop, clip clop,
Clip clop, clip clop, off to town.

5 ~ 4 ~ 3 2 1
This little kangaroo has lots of fun,
First jumps up, and then jumps down,
▲ And then goes jumping off to town.
Boing, boing...

5 ~ 4 ~ 3 2 1
This little spider has lots of fun,
First jumps up, and then jumps down,
▲ And then goes rickle tickle off to town.
Rickle tickle, rickle tickle...

Skip one window

● Walk one window, tidy-o,
Walk one window, tidy-o,
Walk one window, tidy-o,
Jingle at the window, tidy-o.
■ Jing-a-long jing-a-long
Jing-a-long, Joe,
Jingle at the window, tidy-o.

Skip one window, tidy-o...
Jing-a-long jing-a-long...

Trot one window, tidy-o...
Jing-a-long jing-a-long...

Jump one window, tidy-o...
Jing-a-long jing-a-long...

---

5 ~ 4 ~ 3 2 1

Little babies+
● Jog her on your lap.

■ Jump her up high, then down between your knees.

▲ Click your tongue on 'clip clop' while you jog her; lift her in springy bounces on 'boing'; run tickly fingers all over her on 'rickle tickle'.

Make up your own variations ~ bike, butterfly, elephant...

Toddlers+
She'll love dancing to this and being the animals. Even more fun when you join in.

Skip one window

Little babies+
A spray of bells makes a lovely sound for a baby. During the verses, tap the edge of a bell spray to the speed of:

● walking; skipping; trotting; jumping.

■ In the chorus, tap them at a trot.

Toddlers+
● You can re-energise your tired toddler with this if you and another adult take her hands and swing her along between you.

18

To market

To market, to market,
To buy a fat pig,
Home again, home again,
Jiggety jig.

To market, to market,
To buy a fat hog,
Home again, home again,
Jiggety jog.

To market, to market,
To buy a plum bun,
Home again, home again,
Market is done.

19

Two small dogs

Two small dogs came walking by,
Each one wearing collar and tie,
Two small dogs in brand new suits,
And each one wore four
        wellington boots.
Two small dogs.
Tip tap tip tap on your toes,
Two small dogs with far to go,
Tip tap in your brand new suits,
And tip tap in your
        wellington boots.
Two small dogs.

Two small dogs came back again,
Through the puddles in the rain,
Each small dog had one wet foot,
For each had lost one
        wellington boot.
Two wet dogs.
Spit spat spit spat one wet toe,
Two small dogs with far to go,
Spit spat in your soggy suits,
And spit spat in your
        wellington boots.
Two wet dogs.

Two small dogs

Little babies+
Jog her on your knee.

Tap her ankles
together in time to
the beat.

To market

Little babies+
Bounce her on
your knee at a slow,
walking pace.

Bounce her at a
quick jog.

Fill the rumbly grumbly tum!

Pat-a-cake 20

● Pat-a-cake, pat-a-cake, baker's man,
Bake me a cake as fast as you can.

■ Pat it and prick it,
And mark it with B,

● And put it in the oven for Baby and me.

Sweet potatoes 21

● Soon as we all cook sweet potatoes,
Sweet potatoes, sweet potatoes,
Soon as we all cook sweet potatoes,
Eat 'em right straight up.

Soon as we all skin a banana,
Skin a banana, skin a banana,
Soon as we all skin a banana,
Eat it right straight up.

Soon as we all slice up an apple,
Slice up an apple, slice up an apple,
Soon as we all slice up an apple,
Eat it right straight up.

In with the spoon

Down with the sun, up with the moon,
Out with the cat, and in with the spoon!

The tum drum

Oh, the tum drum, the tum drum,
The rumbly grumbly tum drum,
The tum drum, the tum drum,
The finest drum for me.
   And I shall play the tum drum,
      the round as currant bun drum,
   I shall play the tum drum, the finest drum for me.

The toe tap, the toe tap,
The happy, tappy toe tap,
The toe tap, the toe tap,
The finest tap for me.
   And I shall play the toe tap,
      the give my mum a nap tap,
   I shall play the toe tap, the finest tap for me.

The wave about, the wave about,
The wave my arms around about,
The wave about, the wave about,
The finest wave for me.
   And I shall play the wave about,
      the bend them in and stretch them out,
   I shall play the wave about, the finest wave for me.

In with the spoon

Bigger babies+
A spoonful of fun for a happy tea time: swoop her spoon down, up, around then into her open mouth.

The tum drum

Little babies+
Pat her back to the beat of the song ~ especially helpful when she needs winding.

Bigger babies+
Tap her tummy; tap her feet together; wave her arms.

Stroke her tummy in circles; knead her feet in your hands; flex her arms in and out.

Toddlers+
Make up new actions and sounds, eg 'The hand clap...', 'The knee knock...', 'The nose blow...' (!)

Wipe the jam from
nose and toes

This little pig sidebar

This little pig

Little babies+
- First and second pigs ~ rub her tummy. Third and fourth pigs ~ run your fingers up her chest and press her chin on 'bears'.
- Jar ~ pat tummy firmly. Fifth pig ~ kiss her hand.

Toddlers+
- Lightly pinch each of her fingertips in turn, starting with the little one.
- Clap hands on 'slam slam'. 'Gobble' her thumb on 'jam'.

Fruit salad

Little babies+
- Kiss one of her palms then the other.
- Blow a raspberry on her tummy.

Round and round the garden

Little babies+
- Stroke her tummy in a circle.
- Walk your fingers up her and tickle her chin.

Bigger babies+
- Trace round her palm with your fingertip.
- Step your fingers up her arm and tickle her. (She'll soon love doing it to you.)

This little pig 24

- This little pig had a rub a dub dub,
  This little pig had a scrub a scrub scrub,

  This little pig-a-wig ran upstairs,
  This little pig-a-wig called out BEARS!

- Down came the jar with a loud slam! slam!
  And this little pig ate all the jam.

Fruit salad 25

- Let's eat an apple,
  Let's eat a plum,

- Let's blow a raspberry
  On your tum!

Round and round the garden 26

- Round and round the garden
  Like a teddy bear,

- One step, two steps ~
  TICKLE you under there.

We love baby

We love baby, yes we do,
We love baby, yes we do,
We love baby, yes we do,
Baby is our darling.

Clap, clap, clap your hands,
Clap, clap, clap your hands,
Clap, clap, clap your hands,
Baby is our darling.

Stroke, stroke, stroke your head,
Stroke, stroke, stroke your head,
Stroke, stroke, stroke your head,
Baby is our darling.

Tap, tap, tap your knees,
Tap, tap, tap your knees,
Tap, tap, tap your knees,
Baby is our darling.

Diddle diddle dumpling

Diddle diddle dumpling, my son John
Went to bed with his trousers on.

One shoe off, and one shoe on,
Diddle diddle dumpling, my son John.

We love baby

Little babies+
A back-patting or rocking croon for relaxing before bed time.

Bigger babies+
During the verses: cuddle and rock her; cradle her while you take her hand and clap it lightly with yours; stroke her head; tap her knees.

Kiss or cuddle her.

Diddle diddle dumpling

Little babies+
Walk her feet in the air or pat them together as she lies on her back.

Bigger babies+
Sit with her on your lap, facing outwards. Take an ankle in each of your hands.

Pat her feet together.

Kick each foot a little higher, then pat them together again.

Toddlers+
When she knows it well, miss off the last word in each line ~ she'll soon fill them in herself.

STORY TIME number song

The day I went to sea

All
A lively number song
to dance, rock or
bounce to ~ just in
case there's any
excess energy left at
the end of the day.

29

When I was one I sucked my thumb
The day I went to sea,
I jumped aboard a pirate ship
And the captain said to me ~
I'm going this way that way
Forwards and backways
    over the Irish Sea,
A bottle of rum to fill my tum
And that's the life for me.

When I was two I tapped my shoe
The day I went to sea,
I jumped aboard a pirate ship
And the captain said to me ~
I'm going this way that way
Forwards and backways
    over the Irish Sea,
A bottle of rum to fill my tum
And that's the life for me.

When I was three I scraped my knee
The day I went to sea,
I jumped aboard a pirate ship
And the captain said to me ~
I'm going this way that way
Forwards and backways
    over the Irish Sea,
A bottle of rum to fill my tum
And that's the life for me.